THE HORDE

Published by Dark Titan Publishing. A division of Dark Titan Entertainment.

Also available in eBook.

Dark Titan Extended is a branch of Dark Titan Entertainment.

First Printing 2021.

Paperback ISBN: 978-1-7369944-0-5
eBook ISBN: 978-1-7369944-1-2

darktitanentertainment.com

THE HORDE

TY'RON W. C. ROBINSON II

CONTENTS

CHAPTER ONE

Interstate 5 in Washington state is completely packed. Many are trying to enter Seattle as other drivers try to find their way through. In the front, the drivers notice that a hazard sign has been placed on the interstate for anyone traveling through. No vehicles are moving, just sitting in their current places. One driver, a man, exits his vehicle and proceeds to walk to the front of the interstate. As drivers honk their horns at each other trying to get pass, the man continues walking through.

As he looked closer, he's yanked to the ground. He started to scream as his body is being ripped apart by unseen forces. They bite onto his neck and arms, draining the blood from his body. His screams are heard from the other drivers. As he screamed, other drivers walk out of their vehicles, only to be attacked by the forces as well. Now, the entire interstate is covered with abandoned cars and over a hundred scattered people running for their lives.

The people begin running toward the entrance into downtown Seattle. They continue to run and scream in horror as many of them are being knocked to the ground or yanked behind a vehicle. Many lie on the ground, being ripped apart and bitten in the neck, arms, and thighs. Many are reaching the entrance quickly, but the forces are moving at a faster pace, catching and killing anyone who's in their way.

Inside an office of a home sat Dr. Allan Desportan, a scientist who works on different species of animals and sometimes works on finding cures for diseases. As he sat at his desk, examining a file that contained information about Polio, he looked up at the TV in his office, he noticed it was CNN, which presented a broadcasting the instate event, Desportan leaned in and realized the running people were heading downtown in Seattle. As he watched the live footage, he seen the forces that were chasing and killing the people. Deep pale skin, some with red eyes, glowing from the reflections of light, others with clear eyes and long fanged teeth coming from their mouths.

Desportan stood up from his desk and goes for his white lab-style coat and someone's knocking on his door. He walked to the door and opened it. A Caucasian woman with long wavy black hair. She wore a buttoned-down shirt with blue jeans and looked to be in her late twenties.

"Dr. Seward." Desportan said. "What are you doing here?"

"I came to check to see if you just saw the footage of the interstate."

"I did." I was about to drive near it to examine the creatures."

"I think you shouldn't go." Seward said. "Its best that you stay indoors to avoid this. I'm sure we'll be involved with this tomorrow."

"You have a point there." Desportan said. "Thanks for warning me, Lucy."

"You're my colleague." Lucy said. "I have no choice but to watch out for you."

Lucy left Desportan's home. He walked back inside and sat in his office, still watching the live feed of the interstate. Now, there aren't many people running on the streets, they're just lying on the ground either dead or dying.

"What in God's name is going on."

CHAPTER TWO

In the morning, CNN reports that over one-hundred and fifty casualties were documented in the interstate massacre. Desportan arrives into the public science laboratory in Seattle. Seeing Lucy again, he walked toward her, entering her office.

"Good morning, Lucy."

"Same to you, Doctor."

"So, what's the current situation on the Interstate incident?"

"The bodies have been taken to the morgue. I will contact them in a few about any unusual symptoms to the bodies."

"Very well."

Desportan walked into his office to find an envelope on his desk. He walked over and picked it up. He looked to see who it was from, which was his ex-wife, Eva Desportan. He opened the letter, which was a response about their divorce and what she would receive from it. The letter stated that she demands a BMW be brought to her. He picked up his cell phone and called her.

"Eva, yes its me. I just received your letter about the car."

"What do you mean 'the car'? it's a BMW that you bought me and I want it immediately."

"There are more important things going on right now and I can't get to it at this time."

"You better get to it, because there's nothing more important than me receiving my BMW."

"It'll be a while before you receive it."

"Just bring it to me."

Eva hung up, which Desportan put the phone down.

"She'll never understand."

Lucy walked into Desportan's office. He looked up and seen her.

"Anything major?"

"The bodies at the morgue. They all have bites marks on their throats, arms, and legs."

"Bite marks?"

"The coroner's not sure as to what caused those bites."

In the Museum of History and Industry, a man is currently walking through. He is German doctor, a fellow historian and he's also a vampire hunter. He is known as Professor Abelard Ekkehardt. Abelard scans the aisle for anything related to vampirism or any source that connects to vampires. As he approaches the final set of aisles on the row, finding a book related to vampirism. He sits at a table in a corner as he scans through the book quickly. He stopped at one particular page, which showed an illustration of a horde of vampires.

Abelard squinted his eyes at the pack and thought back about the interstate incident. Abelard knows that vampires are the cause of the interstate disaster. Abelard leaves the museum. Abelard arrived at the hospital which has the bodies of the deceased in their morgue. He walked toward the receptionist's desk.

"Excuse me, I would like to speak with your coroner, please."

"I'm not sure if I can allow something like that."

"Please, madam. It's of a serious matter. The bodies are not safe to be examined on."

The receptionist cautiously points to the direction of the morgue. Abelard looked and thanked her. He moved quickly through the amount of people in the hallways. He turned two corners before reaching a door that says "Morgue" on its nameplate.

"Finally."

Abelard walked into the morgue and seen firsthand the number of bodies lying inside. He spotted the bite marks.

"Dear God."

The door opened behind him and it's the coroner. Abelard

walked up to him and pointed at the bodies.

"What are you doing in here, sir?"

"Please, you must listen to me. You need to rid of these bodies and burn them immediately! They're not safe to be around."

"Why don't I just call security to see if you're alright."

"I am alright! I've been doing this job for over thirty years. I know when a body should not be messed with and you're trailing on some thin ice here, young man."

Abelard walked to the door, before exiting the morgue, he turned to the coroner with a concerned look on his face.

"Please, burn the bodies. All of them."

Abelard walked out of the morgue and exited the hospital. The coroner walked out to see if Abelard left. As he stood at the door, a doctor passed by, looking the same direction.

"What was the problem?"

"Just some crazy old man, that's all."

After the moon set, a group of vampires, some with hair, others bald. All of them are pale and have clear eyes and razor sharp teeth. Others have some sort of ooze coming from their mouths. Over a dozen of them gathered at Crown Hill Cemetery. The dozen vampires move quickly to a grave site. The grave dug opened. The vampires sit or stand in an orderly fashion. They seem to be waiting for something or someone. A few begin to hear someone walking over to them. A tall force, wearing all black with black hair and pale eyes. He even had a pair of sharp teeth of his own with sharp nails. He stood above the dozen vampires as they bowed before him. The tall force raised his arms.

"My children. I am Dunkan, The Dark One. Your lord and master."

The vampires cheer at Dunkan. Praising him as their God.

"I have gathered you all here on this night to pass down a message of The Fated Ones. We shall transform this city into our homeland. The interstate was just the beginning as we much kill as many as we can. Whether they're man, woman, or child, we must make a stand here and claim it as our own. Once we claim this city, we'll travel south to claim more. After a few months, we'll have this entire country and within a year, we'll have the whole world at our disposal."

The vampires cheer with sounds of snarls and growls. Dunkan smiled down at them, loving the attention he was receiving.

"We must fully take command and give praise to The Fated Ones. For if not for them, I would not be standing in front of you today to give you this message. We must stand tall and we must conquer all!"

All the vampires screech in praise. Dunkan walked away, looking back one time with a huge smile on his face.

CHAPTER THREE

The next day, as Abelard and Lucy were sitting in the office, discussing the bodies in the morgue, Abelard appeared immediately and approached Desportan's office. Desportan and Lucy get up from their chairs and stood up, facing Abelard.

"Excuse me, doctor. I need to deliver a very important message here."

"What would that message be? If I may ask?" Desportan said.

"Burn the bodies that are lying in the morgue. They're not safe."

"What do you mean they're not safe?" Lucy said.

"The bite marks on the bodies from the interstate. They're not what they seem to be. An animal did no such thing. You're dealing with a much threatening force."

"What are you talking about, sir?"

"I sense that you wouldn't believe me even if I told you."

Desportan sits at his desk, Lucy sat back down. They allow Abelard to sit in front of the desk.

"Please, tell us."

"What you're dealing with, they're cold-blooded, threatening, terrifying, and bloodthirsty. I'll just tell you that they're vampires."

Desportan turned to Lucy. No word from his mouth.

"Vampires?" Lucy said.

"Yes ma'am. Vampires. I know it seems hard to believe, but I am telling you the truth. Those bodies must be burned immediately. They only have one more night before they fully turn."

"I don't fully understand." Desportan said.

"I am aware of that, doctor. So, what are the two of you going to do about it?"

Desportan turned to Lucy. Not knowing what they could do. He paused and looked at Abelard. He nodded his head.

"Could you tell us more about these vampires, as you call them."

"I sure can."

Abelard pulled out a book from his coat and opened it. He turned from page to page. He stopped at one page and handed the book to Desportan. He put on his reading glasses and looked at the book. Lucy stood up behind him, looking in the book as well. Desportan is confused as to what he's currently reading.

"This cannot be possible to exist." Desportan said.

"They do, sir. They exist among us."

"How did you discover all of this?" Lucy said.

"Because I am a vampire hunter from a land far away. I'll tell you more about that later. But, for right now, we must focus on what is here in Seattle."

Desportan read the book and noticed the title *"v12 Virus"*. He looked at Abelard, turning the book around for Abelard to see. Abelard sees it and smiled. He could tell the doctor was interested.

"What the hell is a v12 virus?"

"The v12 virus. That particular strain is what created the vampires in today's time. They appeared to be a mixture of certain viruses that are commonly spoken of across vampire folklore. Noteworthy are the *v5* and *Blood Fire* viruses. After some thought and examinations, it appears the v12 virus is the strongest and most contagious out of the three virus strains. However, it takes a much longer time span for the virus to fully spread throughout the human body."

"I've heard of those two viruses." Desportan said. "I'm fully aware of those two."

CHAPTER FOUR

Desportan handed the book back to Abelard. Abelard takes the book and places it back into his coat pocket.

"So, what are you going to do about those bodies?"

"I'll talk with Lucy about it and we'll come up with a decision."

Abelard smiled.

"That's fortunate enough to hear."

"Though, I would like for you to leave this office. Don't want to have security come up here asking questions."

"Fair enough."

Abelard walked out of the office. Desportan called Abelard back into the office. Abelard stood by the door, waiting for Desportan's response.

"We can talk at lunch. At the café. Once there, you can tell me everything."

"Very well. I'll meet you there, doctor."

Abelard left the office. Lucy turned to Desportan as she sat in the chair in front of the desk. Desportan sits quietly thinking to himself of what he just read and what he heard from Abelard.

"You're not seriously taking this all in."

"What if that man was telling the truth. The bite marks had to come from something and there were no animals reported at the interstate that night."

"Animals could've been there. The interstate was right next to an opening where dogs or cats could've came over. I can't take this vampire tale seriously enough to believe it."

"I understand where you're coming from, Lucy. I get the

whole picture here."

Desportan stood up from his chair and stood by the window, looking out over Seattle.

"I'll meet with him at the café to see what else he has to say. I have to be sure on this one."

Later that day, Desportan meets with Abelard at the café. They shake hands as Desportan sits at the table.

"I never got your name." Desportan said.

"I am Professor Abelard Ekkehardt. I'm from Romania."

"I'm Dr. Allan Desportan. So, what are you doing in America?"

"I was doing some research about the country and I was about to leave the country until the interstate incident."

"What more could you tell me about these vampires?"

Abelard pulled out more books, a map, and medical reports containing information about the vampires. Desportan looked at the books. They appeared to be a century year old.

He scanned the map that showed locations where vampires have been throughout the world, and he started to read the medical reports.

"If I may ask, where did you get all of these?"

"While I am a professor, I am also a vampire hunter. I did most of my hunting across Romania and parts of Germany."

Desportan continued reading the medical files. He is stunned by its accuracy and how they also give references to the v5 and Blood Fire viruses.

"The v5 and Blood Fire viruses exist, according to these reports."

"Yes they do. Apparently, the theory says that when both viruses are combined, they create the v12 virus."

"That's hard enough to hear. I'm still believing that vampires don't exist. Yet, I'm reading files that contain concrete references to their existence."

"It's hard for a first-time believer to accept these things. It happens a lot in my field."

"That's good enough to hear."

Desportan's cell phone rings. He looked and saw Lucy. He

answered it.

"Lucy, what is it?"

"The bodies that were in the morgue are gone. Every last one of them that were from the interstate."

"What of the coroners?"

"They're dead. Bites marks on them as well in all the same places. Maybe that doctor wasn't crazy after all."

"That's exactly what I was thinking. Keep me updated."

Desportan put his phone back into his pocket. Abelard looked at him, wondering what the call was about.

"So, what did she tell you?"

"The bodies are gone and the coroners are dead."

"Already? It can't be. They only had one more night before they fully turned."

"Maybe, that virus has been updated to spread faster."

"We must get prepared, immediately."

Desportan stared at Abelard. He can't even think.

"What do you mean prepared? Prepare for what?"

"This is a sign of a war. A war is coming and we must get prepared."

"What kind of war?"

"The End War. The war that is slated to end all humanity on this planet, so vampires can have it for themselves."

Abelard stood up and packed his bag. Desportan looked at him, concerned about what to say or do.

"What should I do if its as bad as you're saying it is?"

"Pack all of your gear. Your medicines, your tools and find some weapons that you can use. Because you're going to need them very soon to defend yourself."

Abelard left the café as Desportan drinks the last of his coffee.

CHAPTER FIVE

A group of drug dealers sit within an alleyway in the midlevel areas of Seattle. They're discussing the drug trade of shipments that haven't arrived at the proposed due date. One of the dealers began to threaten the others, demanding that he have his shipment in by the morning. As they talked, a man, wearing a black jacket and jeans with a hood over his head, covering his face, walked in between them. The dealers stare at him intensely, believing he's a spy for another dealer or a cop.

"Hey, what's your problem here?"

The man continued to walk past them. One dealers jerks the man by his jacket and slammed him into the brick wall. Looking him in the face, he asked the man the same question again and he received no response. They notice they can't see the man's face due to the hood. The dealer reached for the hood. Above them are a group of vampires, sitting quietly on the roof, watching the dealers in the alley. The dealer placed his hand on the hood and pulled it off.

"What the hell."

The dealer stared in the eyes of the man. His skin pale, eyes a clear gray, and sharp fangs. The man screeches at the dealer before lunging on his neck, biting into him. The other dealers try to run out of the alley but surrounded by more of the vampires. The vampires snarl and screech before attacking the other dealers. Killing them instantly their fangs went into their throats. The blood draining from the bodies as water would drain from a pipe.

In the morning, Desportan reads a newspaper on his desk. The front cover of the newspaper reveals the dealers that were killed in the alley. The most focused detail within the article are the bites marks that were seen on the dealers' throats, arms, and legs. He placed the newspaper on his desk, looking outside his window. As he turned around, Abelard entered his office.

"So, I take it you heard about those drug dealers in the alley."

"It doesn't prove anything except they were murdered."

"By vampires. The bites marks confirm that theory. We must warn the citizens, get them prepared and protected."

"We can't do that, it would start a panic in the city, causing more harm than good."

Abelard nodded before walking towards the door. He turned back, looking at Desportan. He smiled.

"I have a suggestion."

"Name it."

"What if you and I head out to that alley this very night. Look for sources and traces ourselves. That way, if we do stumble upon something, it will prove to you that everything I've told you and telling you is true."

"I'm not allowed to go to the crime scene. Let alone take someone who's not a member of the force."

"Just take my word this one time, doctor. Let me prove to you that vampires exist."

Desportan gets up from his desk and walked over to Abelard.

"Very well, I'll tag along with you tonight to investigate. But, don't cause any damage to the crime scene."

Abelard walked out of the office. Desportan sits back at his desk as Lucy looks on toward him. She knows that he won't listen to her about ignoring the possibility of vampires living in Seattle. So, she returned to her office and stayed quiet.

Meanwhile, inside an abandoned tunnel of a railway station, Dunkan gathered the vampires among him into the railway. He looked at each of the vampires, smiling at how animalistic and vicious they have become recently. Some of the vampires are in fact victims of the interstate incident, clothes torn and dirty. Others with their clothing drenched with blood. Theirs and others.

"Our time is not far away as the humans believe. Once, we take this city by surprise, we'll take the country and the world. We must achieve the goal of The Fated Ones, no matter the sacrifices or mistakes. The Fated Ones must be worshipped and after we've taken over this decadent land, The Fated Ones will rise again to reclaim this world as their own. With you as their soldiers, they will be unstoppable at their cause to reshape Earth into a shadowed land."

CHAPTER SIX

As night fell, Desportan and Abelard travel to the interstate to look for any other signs of vampires. While they search, Desportan stared to ask Abelard questions concerning the vampires' existence and how he's well known of it.

"I'm well aware of vampires because they mainly appeared in across decades. For example, during the end of the World Wars, mostly World War II, vampire sightings were increased expediently in small villages. Quieter. Less noise. Frightening many Europeans across the country more than those of Stalin or Hitler would have done. I took it upon myself to fight off those dreadful creatures and save my homeland. Not for the duty of the War, only to do my part in protecting my people."

"So, were they involved with many world events? Possible experimentations?"

"They weren't experiments. The war was more talked about than the vampires. Even though the vampires would feed on the desperate people within the concentration camps and villages. I fought as many as I possibly could to save as many as possible. All of the land was polluted by the evil which lurked."

"Sorry to hear about that."

"Funny thing is after the war ended, the vampires disappeared. Ever since, any war that was started in any corner of the world, the vampires would be there. Whether the wars were civil or global, the vampires were there. It seemed they were attracted to warfare or even conjured up somehow through possible occults."

After finding no traces to vampires on the interstate, they travel to the alleyway. Within the alleyway there were no signs of the murdered drug dealers. As they proceeded to enter the alleyway. Abelard started to feel uncomfortable, which caught Desportan's attention.

"Are you alright, professor?"

"I'm well. I sense a presence among us and it isn't a friendly one. We must hurry this quickly."

Abelard reached into his coat pocket and pulled out two standard revolvers. He handed one to Desportan, who took it slowly.

"You ever use one of these before, Desportan?"

"I've used a gun before, but never a revolver."

"Their filled with silver bullets. So, watch your every move as possible."

"You're telling me that silver bullets are the only thing that can kill a vampire?"

"You ask so many questions for a novice in this field, doctor. There are other things that can kill a vampire, I only have those bullets currently."

"Good to know."

They entered the alleyway. Its darker than it was before with only a few inches of light shining in from the buildings nearby or the moon above. While, walking through the alleyway, Abelard looked down at his feet and noticed a large amount of dried blood. He gets Desportan's attention and points down at the blood.

"We need to take some of this blood. Could be some traces of vampire venom within it. Just to make sure."

As light shined through the alley, it touched the blood, causing it to glow a greenish color. Abelard pulled out a cloth and rubbed it against the pavement. Getting much of the blood onto the cloth, Desportan takes out a plastic bag as Abelard placed it inside.

"I'm sure you and your lady friend can do some tests on that blood. It could definitely be a key to the vampires."

Desportan placed the bag in his pocket. Suddenly, they hear something scurrying in front of them at the other side of the alley. Desportan slowly reached into his pocket for the revolver as Abelard pulled out a flashlight. He points toward the end of the alleyway. They moved closer and Abelard hears the sound coming from a trashcan nearby. They move towards the trashcan to only reveal a possum. It runs past them and out of the alleyway, moving left into the sidewalks.

"We had to be sure."

They prepare to leave the alleyway since there was no hard sign of a vampire. As Abelard turned around, a vampire jumped in front of them. Pale skin, red eyes, and an extensive amount of hair loss. He snarls at Abelard and Desportan, revealing its elongated fangs.

"Desportan, shoot it!"

Desportan fired a shot at the vampire, it dodges the bullet quickly, moving in a pace to which Desportan and Abelard moved very slowly. The vampire jumped onto the wall, snarling at Abelard. Abelard pulled out his revolver and fired at the vampire three consecutive times. The first two shots were dodged by the vampire, but the third shot hit's the vampire through its head. The vampire's body falls to the ground, motionless.

"Nice shot."

"I had to do something because you missed."

Desportan kneeled down by the body, beginning to examine it. Abelard noticed Desportan's reaction and behavior concerning the vampire. He's seen such responses in the past. Much in similar detail. He never surprises him. Desportan was in total focus, looking at the body.

"I suggest we take this back to your lab so you can examine it there instead of in a crime spot. Unless you want the police to find us here and bring us in for questioning. Just a thought."

"Good idea." Desportan replied. "Lucy can help us with this."

"Will she?"

"We'll see."

They pick up the vampire's corpse and place it inside

Desportan's car, heading to the lab for the study.

CHAPTER SEVEN

Desportan and Abelard enter the lab with only Lucy inside. They're carrying the vampire corpse with them. Lucy watched as they brought the body into the morgue area of the lab.

Inside the morgue, Lucy slowly moved toward the body and noticed its pale skin and elongated fangs. She turned to Desportan with an uncertain look upon her face. She started to shake her head in disbelief.

"This can't be real."

"Well, it is." Desportan said.

"Now, do you truly believe, doctor?" Abelard asked.

Desportan only gave a nod. Abelard nodded back.

"I see. This means you will continue in your efforts to end this before Seattle is fully consumed?"

"Consumed?" Lucy said. "What do you mean?"

"He means before everyone in the city is turned into whatever these things are."

Looking closer, Lucy realized the body was dehydrated, pointing toward the veins and the arteries. Desportan approached the table, staring at the dried veins. Abelard sighed.

"What is this?" Desportan asked.

"There's no blood flowing through the body." Lucy answered. "None. Not even an inch. Somehow, this body was drained prior to the transformation."

"Because another vampire drank from this poor soul." Abelard said.

"Drink?" Desportan asked. "Like drink-drink?"

"How else do vampires consume the blood of their victims."

"Then, how did this person become one of them?" Lucy questioned. "I'm not understanding any of this."

"When the vampire bites into the victim, not only does it drain the blood, but it injects a parasite, if you will, a venomous parasite which travels from the neck to the heart. From there, the blood is fully drained, and the transformation begins. Sometimes quick and other times slow. It all depends on the health of the victim's body."

"And you've seen this before?" Desportan asked. "All of it?"

"Yes. Why else would I be here talking to either of you."

Desportan sighed, walking toward one of the seats, sitting down, holding his head.

"I see the woof you have some adjustments to do on your beliefs as to what's real and what isn't." Abelard spoke. "However, now isn't the time. By this rate after what we encountered, there has to be around a dozen of them already in the city. Underground most likely and we need to find them now. Before they come up and scatter through the city like rats."

"How far could they be underground?" Desportan asked. "Maybe they're hiding out in the sewers."

"Not if sunlight is beaming through the tops." Abelard replied. "They go deeper. They always do."

Lucy walked over toward the desk, digging through the drawers. In the second one, she pulled out a map and laid it out. Gazing across the map of the city and its underground layers, she pointed toward a particular spot. She called Desportan and Abelard over to the table where they came and saw.

"Perhaps here." She pointed. "The Central Link Station."

Desportan nodded.

"Let's give it a shot."

"Ready when you are." Abelard said.

"Then let's get going." Desportan replied. "Lucy, myself and Abelard will head out. I would like for you to stay here."

"Stay here? You need as many hands if you come across any trouble. Much less anything else."

"It's better you stay here. You can learn more about their biology. That way, you can find a way for us to face them head-on."

"Silver is for that." Abelard said.

Desportan gave Abelard a look. Abelard nodded with a grin.

"Just stay here, keep yourself safe. Me and Abelard will be fine."

"We will." Abelard said. "Trust us."

Lucy sighed with a slow nod.

"Go. See what you can find."

"We won't be long." Desportan replied.

They left the lab as Lucy returned to the table, continuing the study of the body.

CHAPTER EIGHT

Desportan and Abelard walked through the Line 1 Light Rail Station, moving through the crowds. Desportan found it strange to have so many people crowded in the station at the time of night. Abelard didn't mind it, the people were enough of a shield in case a vampire had emerged from around them. The crowd would give Abelard the opportunity to strike unseen.

"See anything?" Desportan asked.

"Only the people in front of us, behind us, and all around." Abelard replied. "What of your end?"

"Same."

Both move through the corridors, continuing to bump into the civilians. Desportan is still processing the amount of people moving through the area as Abelard moved with haste, searching throughout the corridors. He stopped, staring toward one and pointed. Desportan walked over to him, seeing Abelard pointing at a sign.

"This corridor is abandoned. Out of use."

"You think this may be the spot?" Desportan questioned. "Perhaps, they're dwelling in there."

"Only way to find out is to walk in ourselves."

They step forward, heading towards the corridor. Yet, in their path arrive two police officers. The officers stand in front of them, blocking their path into the corridor. The officers look at them, searching them. Desportan nodded as he pulled out his ID. Abelard stood steady. Calm. Collective.

"Sorry gentlemen, but this area is closed off to the public."

"Are you sure?" Abelard asked. "Because, me and my

associate here have some business to attend to in this particular corridor."

"I'm afraid you or your colleague have no entry into this section of the station. Otherwise, you'll have to talk to services."

"Look, I understand you cannot let civilians pass through, but this is an emergency. I'm a scientist and what we're working on may have some significant inside that corridor. It's hard to explain, but you have to trust us. We're not here to cause any harm. Just looking for answers."

The officer turned and looked at his partner, who only nodded his head with a smirk. The officer looked back to Desportan and Abelard and nodded.

"Sorry. Can't let you pass."

"I'm telling you, we have to go in there and search for answers. What's going on in this city is a hazard to everyone. Potentially the entire country and you're blocking our path to find a source to the cause?"

"I don't follow your orders, sir. Now turn around and walk away."

"Just let us pass and we'll be gone before you can count to fifty."

"No can do." The other officer said. "Now, you heard my partner. Turn around and head on home."

Desportan nodded, putting his ID back in his pocket. He nodded again and shook his head, turning around to walk away. Abelard watched Desportan leave and he looked back at the two officers and sighed.

"I understand he's keen on getting to the problem to save the people. However, you have orders of your own to follow and I respect an honest man. Yet, what is happening in this city is beyond either of our hands. By declining us entry into that corridor, you may have let loose a terror this world hasn't seen since the Middle Ages. Now, what comes over this city will be on your hands and yours alone."

The officers paused, giving one another a confused, twisted look. Abelard nodded as he turned away.

"Good night to you both."

CHAPTER NINE

Several days had passed with no signs of vampire sightings, which all seemed a bit strange for Abelard to comprehend. Meanwhile, the news began to release reports of a woman moving throughout Seattle claiming to have been killing vampires within the city. The woman was described as a dark-haired sword-wielding huntress who's sole goal was to eradicate the vampires from the city. Abelard and Desportan were inside the lab alongside Lucy as the saw the news on the TV. Abelard nodded with a smirk.

"Seems we're not the only ones out here doing the work."

"I take it you want to find her?" Desportan asked. "Have her join us in this endeavor."

"Exactly. What else will she be of sue besides slaughtering vampires."

"So, how do we contact her? Send out a signal only she will understand? Hopefully."

"We call her out."

"No one knows who she is." Lucy said. "Not even her name."

"That is something we'll discover ourselves." Abelard replied. "No need to wait on the news to inform us of details we surely need."

"Still doesn't answer how we'll track her down."

"I have one." Abelard said. "It'll be a simple task."

"How simple?" Desportan questioned.

Abelard and Desportan traveled out to the City Park. There,

Abelard sat down as Desportan gazed the surroundings. Seeing people casually out during the day. No fear in the air nor any paranoia. Desportan found it comforting, however Abelard felt sadness as to what may come.

"I'm not certain as to what we're supposed to be looking for."

"Give it a minute." Abelard said. "You'll catch someone acting strange within a second."

"How strange?"

"Strange enough to get some eyes on them."

Desportan nodded with uncertainty. He continue looking around. Abelard kept his eyes focused on the field in front of him. Checking his pocket, Abelard caught a glimpse of something in the corner of his eye. He grinned. Looking to his right side, seeing a woman sitting next to him.

"Good to see you noticed." Abelard said.

Desportan turned around to see who Abelard was speaking to and saw the woman sitting beside him.

"You looked strange just sitting out here." She said. "As did your friend standing there gawking around like a stalker."

"I'm not a stalker. I'm a scientist."

"You look like one."

"I take it you're the woman who was on the news today. Going around slaughtering vampires?"

"Truth be told, I did what had to be done."

"So it is you?" Desportan asked. "You're the huntress."

"Huntress? Funny. Never thought of myself as one."

"Good to finally meet you. Abelard Ekkehardt."

"Anna Ilario."

Desportan looked at Anna's attire. Seeing it's mostly all leather with violet highlights layered throughout. Her long dark hair is what strikes the most from her appearance as did her blue eyes.

"Why seek me out?"

"Because we share a similar goal. I've spent most of my life hunting down vampires and sometimes other nasty creatures. After seeing the news and hearing about your work, I must ask if you will aid us."

"Aid you in taking out the vamps? I'm sure you two can

handle them yourselves. I'll just continue to do what I do."

"Do you know that these vampires have a master? That it is he who sends them out to do his bidding?"

"Like some kind of warlord vampire?"

"More so." Abelard nodded. "I get going around the city killing any vampire in your sights is doing swift justice. I know. But, there is more to their existence and to this work. Much more."

Anna nodded. She looked at Abelard's side, seeing he's holding onto something tightly.

"What's under the coat?"

"My choice of weaponry." Abelard answered, showing his blade.

"Not bad." Anna smiled.

"No need to show me yours. I'm aware of your sword-wielding achievements."

"By achievements, you mean kills."

"Precisely. So, will you be joining us on this hunt?"

"If it means protecting the innocent in this city, then I'm all in."

"Good. But, remember this. It's not only Seattle you're fighting to save. It's the entire world."

Anna nodded slightly. She let out a sigh, gazing at the park.

"Are we going to be enough?"

Abelard cocked his head. He let out a faint grin.

"Time will tell. Right now, we need to find out where they're keeping themselves hidden."

"Well, I know a place." Anna said.

Desportan stepped forward. His ears were keen to her next words.

"Where is this place?" Abelard asked.

"First Hill is where I came across them. Still, I see them roaming through the area during the night. Perhaps, they're coming from the hospital. Maybe underground."

"What hospital do you speak of?"

"She's talking about Harborview." Desportan replied. "Harborview is the place."

Abelard stood up from the seat, Anna followed.

"Very well. Let's head to this hospital."

"Wait." Desportan said. "You just want to go there now and do what? Slay the vampires you come across?"

"If it comes to pass, yes."

"But, it's noon. Nightfall isn't here for a few hours."

"Better we head to the hospital and warn the people. That way, the place can be clear for us to continue our work."

"What if they don't believe us?" Anna wondered. "What then?"

"Then we give them a farewell and leave them to their fates. Otherwise, we'll intercede at the proper time."

They agreed and headed on out to Harborview Medical Center. Abelard rushed inside with Anna stepping beside him. Desportan walked in afterwards, greeting the people as Abelard stood in the middle of the lobby, gathering everyone's attention with a yell. The doctors turned to him, making their way toward him Anna stood back, but steady.

"Is something wrong, sir?"

"Yes. You and your colleagues need to evacuate this hospital immediately."

"Why would we do that?"

Abelard sighed, looking over to Anna. She nodded.

"There's a plague somewhere around this place. In order for you not to get caught, you must leave. Return home or wherever you go. Protect yourselves."

"Listen, we're doctors. I'm sure we can handle this matter ourselves."

"This is beyond natural remedies. Only swift justice can cure the world of this plague."

The doctor closed her eyes and turned to Anna.

"Is he ok?"

"I know it's difficult to fathom. But, he's telling the truth. Everyone needs to leave this hospital before dark."

"What of the patients?"

"Take them to another hospital. I know you can transfer them."

"I'm afraid we can't. many rooms are already full. This is the only place to keep them."

"By staying here, you are putting yourselves in serious danger." Abelard said. "I get my words sound like a horror's tale. However, it is the truth. All of it. Creatures beyond human understanding have settled themselves in this city and many have been seen around this hospital. Hence why we're here today."

The doctor nodded and walked over to the desk, speaking to the receptionist. Their voices were low. Desportan remained by the door, watching all who passed by and walked through the lobby. Anna kept her eyes on the desk, seeing the eyes gazing around from the receptionist.

"We need to leave."

"Why?" Abelard asked.

"Because they're calling security. We have to go."

Abelard grunted, approaching the desk. Coming closer, he slammed his hand on the desk, startling the doctor and receptionist. Hearing footsteps from the hall in front of him, Abelard saw three security guards.

"This is what you do. Call security on those who are trying to save your lives?!"

"Sir, you need to leave. Now."

"I'm trying to warn you of the danger which lurks here!"

"Either you leave on your own or by taken in by security. Your choice."

Abelard sighed, looking at the doctors sanding in the lobby as the security arrived. Abelard held his hands up and turned back toward the door. Making his leave. Anna followed him with Desportan last to leave.

Elsewhere, back at the Link Station, one of the tracks had been placed into construction after an apparent faulty track. The construction workers arrived at the station and went quickly into the work of replacing the track. While working, one of the workers caught the sound of a creaking in the distance. He looked into the direction of the sound as it lowered itself. From the creaking came the screeches. Curiosity grew in the worker's mind as he made his way into the corridor. Finding it in a deep darkness. He turned on the flashlight attached to his helmet and turned around to call his collogues, yet the screeches grew louder. The worker went deeper into the corridor and eventually found nothing. Sighing to himself.

"What is that?" He asked.

Turning around to return to the work, the screech echoed through the dark corridor once again. Only this one came from above. The worker stopped in his steps and raised his head to the ceiling, only to find a strange pale-like fluid dripping down on his helmet and shoulders. He wiped it off and as he did, the screech clicked above. The worker looked up and saw a figure latched onto the ceiling. The quickening of fear grew in him as the glowing red eyes froze him. The creature snarled and leaped onto the worker, taking a bite out of his neck and drinking the flowing blood. The worker's cry for help muted into the darkness of the corridor. Turning into silence.

CHAPTER TEN

Desportan and Abelard bring Anna back with them to the office where she is greeted by Lucy while glancing over at the operation room next door, seeing the vampire body. She pointed.

"You guys caught one?"

"Not exactly." Desportan answered. "Just an opportunistic event."

"So, what have you found so far?" Lucy asked.

"Anna here has told us she's come into contact with the vampires around Harborview." Abelard said.

"Did you guys head over there? Just to see for yourself?"

"We did." Desportan answered. "However, the doctors there didn't take our words seriously."

"They wanted us out." Abelard added. "Went as far as calling security to escort us."

"But, that's not going to stop us." Anna said. "I have an idea."

"And what might that idea be?" Desportan questioned.

"Yes." Abelard said. "I am eager to know."

"We, could, you know, head out there by nightfall. Once the vamps make themselves known, we take them out. All in one swoop."

Desportan scoffed, Lucy shook her head, and Abelard nodded silently.

"That's suicide." Desportan said.

"Do you have a death wish or something?" Lucy wondered.

"Straightforward." Abelard said. "I like it. But, it's too much of a risk. Can't take it."

"It's a start at least." Anna sighed.

While they continued speaking, Lucy looked over toward the shelf toward the TV, seeing the news broadcast speaking about the Link Station. She stopped the conversation, pointing towards the TV. Desportan and Abelard looked on as the news unveiled the mysterious murder of one of the construction workers. Abelard knew what killed the worker. He looked over toward Desportan. He knew too. Lucy turned off the TV after the broadcast was finished. She sighed. Anna took a moment to think and snapped her fingers.

"We should go there."

"Been there already." Desportan said.

"Looks like we're going back." Abelard said. "Won't we?"

Desportan stared, rubbing his head.

"We have no choice. We can find the source ourselves. Even though the police might try to block us again."

"No. Don't worry about them. They can't tell us anything after this. No chance."

"Wait, you two went there already?" Anna asked.

"Before the murder." Abelard answered. "We tried to tell the police. They didn't listen."

"I'm tagging along." Anna said. "You'll need another member to join you."

"Then I'm going too." Lucy said.

"Lucy," Desportan replied. "It's better you stay here."

"And why is that?"

"Because if you discover something else related to these things, you can give us an advantage."

"It's better we head there by nightfall." Abelard said.

"What? Why?" Desportan questioned. "We can go there now while there's still sunlight."

"If we do, we won't be able to track down the vampires correctly."

"Correctly? You're sounding like Anna now."

"It's a start at least." Anna responded.

"Very well." Abelard said, standing up from his seat. "I'm ready whoever you are."

"You know what?" Desportan said. "You two go and look. I'll

stay here with Lucy."

Abelard stood by the door as Anna walked through. Abelard stepped one foot out as he turned back to Desportan. Looking to be sure he made his decision. Desportan simply nodded and it was all Abelard needed and he exited the office. Desportan turned toward Lucy and she only looked back between the door and Desportan.

"Allan, are you sure you want to stay here?"

"Abelard and Anna can take care of themselves. Right now, it's best we stay here and see what more we can learn. Now, what have you discovered so far?"

"Nothing besides what we already know."

Desportan grinned with a nod.

"So far, it's all we know about these things."

"Yes."

Desportan reached into his pocket, pulling out his phone. What he saw was a text. He opened and read the message and shook his head. Lucy noticed it bothered him.

"What is it?"

"It's Eva. She wants to meet with me at the bookstore."

"Right now? During all of this?"

"Don't worry. I'll get through it smoothly." Desportan walked toward the exit door. "I'll be back."

"Be safe."

Abelard and Anna arrived at the station, finding it covered with police and forensic scientists. Abelard liked the scenery as Anna was hesitant to make the move forward. Abelard calmed her as they entered the station. Seeing officers speaking to one another as well as several civilians going about through the station. Abelard walked with Anna, pointing toward the corridor.

"That's the one."

"Yes. We have ourselves a little problem." Anna said, seeing two officers standing by the corridor entry.

Abelard remembered the previous encounter, yet, it didn't bother him as he moved forward, approaching the officers. Anna stood with him as the officers looked, seeing them approaching.

"I thought we already told you no entry."

"Yes. You did. However this isn't the time to hold someone back. I have knowledge as to what's dwelling inside that corridor. I know what killed the worker."

"You do?" the officer said. "Then, elaborate for us what killed him?"

Abelard sighed.

"He was killed by a vampire."

"A vampire? Where are you getting this from? Silly stories?"

"He's telling the truth." Anna said. "The man's not fucking around with this."

"Ma'am, lower your tone."

"I'll lower it when you let us pass."

"I will not allow you to enter. This perimeter is cut from the public."

"You said that last time. I let that slide. Now, since my theory is correct, there is a vampire lurking within the corridor. Maybe even more."

The second officer receives a call and wanders off from the area. Abelard saw it as an opportunity. He made a move forward and the officer placed his hand on Abelard's chest. Anna raised up her sword, holding it near the officer's throat.

"Raise up your gun and you'll be bleeding to death."

"You people are crazy."

"No officer." Abelard replied. "Only the naysayers are crazy."

The officer had no other words to speak. Abelard took the silence as permission, walking past the officer into the corridor. Anna lowered the sword and smirked, bumping the officer as she walked past him. Inside the corridor, they found it covered with more forensic scientists, Anna ducked herself behind several crates. Abelard looked ahead, seeing a strange liquid on the ground. He knelt down to get a closer look. Anna saw him as she peaked from behind the crates.

"What is it?"

Abelard sighed bitterly as he saw the liquid.

"They're here."

Abelard stood up and moved with haste from the corridor, returning near Anna. She could see the fear in his eyes as he moved quickly, even his hands began to shiver.

"What's wrong?" Anna asked. "What is it?"

"We need to get everyone and I mean everyone out of this station right now!"

CHAPTER ELEVEN

Abelard and Anna exited the corridor, seeing the officers and forensics continuing their work. Abelard yelled at them to leave the station. The officers glanced at Abelard and Anna, questioning their business in the station.

"Please listen to me." Abelard said. "This place is not safe. You all need to leave this station now."

"We'll leave once our job is done." The officer replied. "Right now, the work continues."

"No. you're not understanding. The danger is within that corridor. An ancient evil killed the worker and it's coming out to kill more. You must heed my words. Leave this station now!"

Anna looked outside the windows, seeing the night sky looming. She turned to Abelard, who also noticed the sunset. He shook his head, pushing himself from the officers who had surrounded him and Anna. One officer jerked Abelard's arm.

"You seem unsettled."

"Because there is danger here. This young lady and I are leaving before it gets dark. You should do the same. All of you."

"Sir, we need you to calm down."

"I'm calm enough to be aware of my senses."

"We didn't do anything." Anna said. "We're just on our way out."

"Right now, you'll stay put. Both of you."

Abelard stomped his foot, showing his eagerness to escape the station. The officers weren't moved. Anna kept her eyes on the exit as one of the officers took out handcuffs from his pocket.

"These won't do any good." Abelard said. "We all need to

leave this place now!"

The sunset had come, far quicker than Abelard anticipated. It was there he knew something was changing. Both in the city of Seattle and the atmosphere above it. The officer went to place the cuffs on them both, but was caught by the sudden sound of screams echoing from the corridor. The officer paused and looked over to the others. They nodded. The officer removed the first cuff from Abelard's wrist as they reached for their firearms and made their way toward the corridor.

"We need to go!" Anna said.

"Save yourselves!" Abelard yelled to the officers. "Do not enter the corridor! Do not!"

Abelard and Anna made it out of the station, moving toward the car. Once they entered, gunfire streaked through the air, coming from within the station. Abelard looked on, seeing several officers running toward the doors as were the scientists. Behind them, Abelard saw three moving figures. Their speed was far more enhanced. He knew.

"We need to return to the office immediately!"

Anna drove from the station as the night sky covered the city and from the station doors came the vampires. The first three caught the car driving away and they quickly ran after it. Abelard looked at the mirror, seeing the vampires making their way toward them.

"Step on it!" Abelard said.

Anna drove faster as two of the vampires lunged in the air, only to scratch the trunk of the car. The third one managed to leap atop the car and began starching its way on the roof and on the windows. Abelard pulled out his revolver.

"What am I supposed to do?" Anna wondered.

"Keep your eyes on the road. No need to get us killed or wrecked."

Abelard rolled down the window, starling Anna as the

vampires lowered its head directly in front of Abelard's revolver. He pulled the trigger, blowing the head off of the vampire as its body fell from the top of the car to the road. Abelard rolled up the window, wiping the blood from his face with a towel. He nodded while Anna did her best to keep her eyes on the road.

"Problem solved." Abelard said. "For now."

"What now?" Anna questioned.

"Now, we return to the office. Tell Dr. Desportan and Dr. Seward about what we've discovered. Do what we can to warn everyone in the city of the coming days. Because, those days might be this city's last."

Anna drove down the street, entering a small traffic stop. The cars covered the streets. Lines of them. Abelard sighed as he glanced around the area for other vampires. Anna also took a look herself just to be sure. The car had stopped with only other cars in front, beside, and behind them. Abelard looked out of the window, catching what he saw was a shadow. Dodging through the traffic. He sighed slowly.

"We need to move and fast."

Desportan had entered the bookstore where he saw Eva sitting at one of the table with a cup of coffee. He greeted her and sat down. She saw he had other things on his mind. However, she did not care and Desportan already could tell.

"Why did you want to meet me?"

"Because we need to talk about the materialistic things."

"Materialistic things? What are you talking about?"

"I need to know what I'll be taking and what you'll be keeping."

"You contacted me for this? In the middle of all that's going on in the city with the interstate and the findings?"

"Now is the important time to discuss these matters, don't you think?"

"I think not, Eva." Desportan sighed. "What do you want?"

"The car."

"The car? Which car?"

"You know the one. I told you to bring it do me. You haven't"

Desportan shook his head and tossed his hands up in the air.

"You called me to come here just because you want the BMW?"

"Yes. What other reason do we have to meet like this? I want the car. Simple."

"Fine. It's yours."

"Where is it?"

"At the house in the garage."

"Then how'd you get here?"

"My work vehicle. What else would I be driving during a time like this."

Eva nodded.

"Fair point. So, how will I be getting the car?"

Desportan stared, reached into his pocket and handed her the keys to the car. He stood up from the table.

"Contact your friend to take you to the house. You can pick up the car."

Eva looked at the keys while Desportan walked out of the bookstore.

Desportan had returned to the office, seeing Abelard and Anna speaking with Lucy. Abelard turned around as Desportan entered through the door.

"Doctor, you've returned."

"I have. Good to see you two aren't dead."

"It was a matter of our speed over suggestion." Abelard replied. "Anyhow, we were telling Dr. Seward what we learned concerning the station corridor."

"What is it?"

"The vampires are there." Anna said. "Not sure how many to be exact. But, we were chased down by three of them."

"Three?" Desportan said. "Out in the open?"

"As soon as the sun sets, yes." Abelard answered. "Even that is a mystery to me."

"The sunset? How?"

"It set faster than it usual does. As if something or someone was manipulating the clouds or the atmosphere. I'm not sure if it happened but the Dark One is known to possess such abilities."

"By the corridor, you're saying you got through."

"We did." Anna said. "Yet, some of the officers weren't so lucky."

"The three vampires killed them. Right before they chased us down the road. We lost two. I killed the third one."

Desportan nodded.

"That's a good start. So, where do we go from here?"

"We need to warn everyone in the city to evacuate as soon as possible."

"I'm sorry, Mr. Ekkehardt, but we cannot put these innocent people in danger by having another traffic hap on the interstate. Not again."

"You are not aware as to how this began. The interstate was only a ploy for them to enter into the city. They were already heading this direction anyhow. If Interstate 5 was not jammed, the vampires would've arrived possibly yesterday or even today. In total, we would all be in this same place regardless.

"And what are we supposed to do?" Lucy wondered. "Go out there and hunt down any vampires we find?"

Abelard stared.

"Yes."

Back at the station, the electricity is out and from the corridor stepped forward the vampires. Approximately over a dozen. In two single-filed lines. In the middle of them walked out Dunkan the Dark One. He looked out through the windows and grinned.

"This night is the moment. The city shall be ours."

CHAPTER TWELVE

"What did you mean by 'The Dark One'?" Anna questioned.

"The Dark One. Known by the name Dunkan. He is the one responsible for all of this. Every bit of it."

"Is he like a god or something?"

"He believes himself to be. I've only ran into him once. Many, many years ago."

"How long has he been around?"

"A very, very, very long time." Abelard said. "Right now isn't the time for a history lesson. We need to bring the fight to him and end this now."

Desportan and Lucy walked toward the table where Abelard and Anna were sitting.

"So, what's the plan?" Desportan asked.

"We take the battle to them. Find the Dark One and end this."

"And how will we find the vampires?" Lucy questioned. "And this Dark One you've spoken about?"

"We make a return trip to the station. We know they're in there. Perhaps, their leader is dwelling within the corridor along with them."

"Hold on." Desportan said. "I'm not sure that's such a good idea. First, you and Anna say you went there and saw several vampires. Attack the police and even managed to chase you down the road. I'm sorry, but that place is not an option. Choose another."

Abelard nodded, glaring toward Anna, who shrugged.

"Very well. What other alternatives do you have, Doctor?"

"Let's head over to Crown Hill. Find out what we can there. Maybe the vampires travel when necessary. Possibly pertaining to the sunlight directions. If we can find something in that cemetery, it may lead us toward this Dark One."

"I stand by your choice." Abelard said, standing up. "Let's get moving."

The four of them had traveled out to Crown Hill Cemetery, discovering many of the graves were not touched. Yet, while searching Anna looked around and discovered over a dozen graves were opened. The coffins were broken into and the bodies were gone. Desportan nodded as he looked down into the graves.

"So, they've come back from the dead."

"Not as their past selves." Abelard said. "They've become something else."

"This is all the openings we've found out here?" Lucy asked.

"Yes." Anna said. "The other graves are covered. Not even a pile of dirt above them."

"Looks like we hit a dead-end of sorts." Desportan said.

"Indeed. What is the proposed next place?"

"Next place? What other places d you think they may operate?"

"I have an idea." Anna said. "The University."

"Are you sure?" Desportan questioned.

"Yes."

Abelard grinned.

"Only one way to find out. Besides, the guards will be busy with what they discover lurking around in the dark."

Desportan with a hint of hesitance decided to go along with them to the University of Washington. Anna detailed them with several instances regarding the university. She described a sighting of a vampire which occurred the day before the Interstate Incident. The students were told to leave the campus grounds the day after the incident, which caused a stir amongst the university.

Once they arrived at the university, they recognized a strangeness in the air surrounding the university grounds. Finding a way inside, they stumbled upon the interior and immediately find a rugged man dressed in jeans and a brown leather jacket walking through with a shotgun. Anna raised her sword as Desportan and Abelard held up the revolvers.

"Put those things down." The man said. "I'm not one of them."

They lowered the weapons as the man walked into the light from the ceiling.

"Who are you?" Anna asked.

"Brant Wade. Who the hell are you guys?"

"We're on business." Abelard said. "What did you mean by 'one of them'?"

"Those creatures. They're in this university. Moving all throughout it. Ran into several of them back there."

"Any survivors?" Desportan asked.

"None so far. Not in here."

"You should join us. Help us in this fight against them."

"What fight?"

"There's more to all this than many know."

A scurrying sound moved through the hallway, causing them to raise their weapons. From the hallway where Brant came from, rushed out three vampires. They lunged in the air toward them, only to be blown in parts by Brant's shotgun.

"We need to move fast." Abelard said. "They know we're here."

They made their move toward the library. However, standing at the other end was a shifting figure, yet its eyes were red as blood and glowing through the darkness. Abelard paused, aiming his revolver forward.

"What is that?" Desportan said.

"A familiar face."

"It is good to see you still living and breathing, Romanian."

"Same goes to you, Viril."

Viril?" Desportan said. "Who the hell is that?"

"Who am I? I do the bidding for the Dark One. I am his

right-hand. Before you stand before him, you must first come before me."

"I've dealt with your wickedness for a far too long." Abelard replied. "This day shall be your last."

"I believe it not to be the case. My lord, Dunkan will decide such a fate. See you around."

Viril warped into the darkness, unable to be found. Abelard stomped his foot and fired several rounds into the shadows in anger. Desportan walked toward Abelard, who sighed before sitting down at one of the nearby tables.

"Tell me, who is this Dunkan?"

"He's, he's far beyond the vampires we've encountered. He is one of the progenitors of their existence. Dunkan is a member of the Fated Ones, a species of vampiric begins who were eliminated during the Great Flood. Few survived the waters as did the Nephilim. Afterwards, the Fated Ones scattered themselves across the world and disappeared into the shadows. Only to reappear during major events. The Trojan War, the Roman Empire, the Babylonian-Persian war, and many others."

"That explains the World Wars connection."

"Yes. To my knowledge, Dunkan is one of the last ones to remain. The others were killed off centuries ago by other hunters in their own regions."

Lucy approached the table, pointing toward the windows, seeing a hint of sunlight peeking through the clouds.

"We need to get moving."

"Of course." Abelard said. "But, I believe we need to prepare ourselves right now. Because this day we're living in, is truly the beginning of the end."

They exited the university with Brant alongside them and as the doors closed, all of the electricity shut down. Not just in the university but throughout the entire city of Seattle. Streetlights, public locations, all electricity was out. An entire blackout filled Seattle.

"What's happening?" Desportan wondered.

"Dunkan has made his move." Abelard answered. "There are no more delays. This is the day."

CHAPTER THIRTEEN

The sunlight above Seattle suddenly turned into darkness, startling everyone on the city. Abelard looked above as they stood outside of the university. Desportan glared up, seeing the eclipse. He pointed with confusion.

"What's happening?"

"This is all part of his plan." Abelard said. "We have no more time to waste. We must find the Dark One and finish him for good."

"Where will he show up?" Brant asked.

"He'll make himself known for us to find him. This eclipse will bring him out in the open. Alongside his soldiers."

Entering the car, they drove through the streets of Seattle, witnessing many of the civilians being attacked by the roaming vampires. Desportan couldn't believe anything he was seeing. Abelard was focused. Lucy shook her head in pity for the people. Anna wanted to help them, even Brant.

"We can't help them." Abelard said. "Only with the Dark One defeated, may those who live be spared."

"Well, in order to end this Dark One, we have to find out where he is." Desportan said.

"I have an idea." Anna said. "Worth a shot."

"What is it?" Abelard wondered.

Anna told them the idea and without haste, they made the move through the city. Arriving back at Harborview. The car had stopped as they glanced out toward the building. No sign of doctors anywhere. Nor vampires.

"You're sure about this?" Desportan asked.

"I am." Anna replied. "This has to be the spot."

Stepping into the hospital lobby, seeing the bodies of doctors and patients on the floor. Desportan shook his head. Abelard walked through, stepping over the bodies and the blood which was splattered throughout the lobby across the floor, walls, and ceiling. Abelard paused as he caught the faint sound of a screech deeper into the hospital hallway. Holding his revolver steady, he signaled the others to follow him. They walked down the hallway, leading toward the cafeteria where they found themselves staring at a dozen vampires.

"The hell is going on here." Brant said, loading the shotgun.

In the midst of the vampires, stood a much taller one. Abelard raised the revolver as the Dark One.

"The Romanian."

"You remember me." Abelard said. "How interesting."

"This is the day you've been waiting for. To face me like a warrior. As where the many have failed, you seek to be the one."

"And I will be the one. Wicked One!"

Abelard fired a shot, hitting Dunkan in the chest. The Dark One wiped off the blow and disappeared into the shadows of the cafeteria. The vampires snarled as their eyes glowed and their teeth glistened. The team was ready for the fight. Abelard searched through the darkness for Dunkan, shouting his name.

"Abelard, where are you going?!" Desportan yelled.

"He's going to the roof! I must face him!"

Abelard moved through the vampires, shooting them in the heads as he made way for the stairs. Desportan, Lucy, Anna, and Brant took out the remaining vampires as they followed Abelard toward the stairs. He reached them and made his way to the ceiling. Once he stepped foot on the ceiling, he saw Dunkan standing before him, gazing up toward the eclipse and orange burning sky. Abelard reloaded the revolver, clicking it to gain the Dark One's attention.

"Are you ready to fall?" Abelard said.

"Fall? Oh no, Romanian. This day, many will fall. yet, I will not."

Abelard fired another shot, Dunkan dodged the round, swiping the revolver from Abelard's hand. Desportan and the others bolted from the door, seeing Dunkan. Desportan fired a shot, getting the Dark One's attention.

"The Doctor."

Brant moved into the fight, blasting the shotgun across Dunkan's chest. The Dark One stumbled as his robe torn from the shot. Anna and Lucy rushed toward Dunkan, slashing him in the arms with their blades. Desportan picked up Abelard's revolver, handing it back to him. All of them combined used their tools against Dunkan, pushing him further toward the edge of the roof. Abelard turned toward Lucy.

"Do it!" Abelard yelled.

Lucy moved and speared the blade into Dunkan's chest. The Dark One froze in place as his arms grabbed the blade. Abelard looked over to Anna.

"Give me the sword!"

Anna tossed the sword to Abelard as he ram over and severed Dunkan's left arm from his body. The Dark One screeched in pain and Desportan fired one shot, hitting the Dark One in the forehead, causing him to collapse and fall off the roof to the pavement. They moved toward the edge, gazing down as they noticed Dunkan's body was not found. Abelard sighed with anger, placing his revolver into its holster. He returned the sword to Anna. Desportan was lost for words.

"I shot him in the head. He should be dead."

"No. He's not dead as you clearly saw. There's more to all of this. We must find out quickly."

Brant looked out toward the city of Seattle and shook his head. He couldn't believe what he was seeing.

"Hey, guys, what's happening?"

They turned, seeing what Brant was watching. Looking out in the distance, they saw flames and smoke growing from Seattle as the eclipse remained. Desportan turned toward Abelard with fear in his eyes. None of them could explain what was happening, only that the city was in chaos and was slowly burning.

"It all makes sense now." Abelard said.

"What makes sense?" Desportan questioned.

"His return. The vampires. The eclipse. The city burning. This isn't the execution. This is the start of his plan."

"So, what do we do?" Anna asked. "What's next?"

"The prophecy has begun." Abelard answered.

"So, it has begun." Desportan said.

Abelard nodded.

"Prepare yourselves. The fight for our lives, everyone's lives is now at stake. We need more fighters to join us. Now, let's go and find them before everyone in this city is either dead or turned."

ONE MISSION: A SPY SHORT STORY

The sound of two gunshots echoed through the darkness. The end of the hallway was difficult to see through without some form of light. Coming through the dark was a figure. Human-shaped. The figure continued to grow as it made each step forward.

Walking out of the dark area was a spy agent. Lean-figured, dressed in a casual suit with no tie. His focus was keen on the mission. The hallway in front of him had lit up with lights upon the walls and the rooms are closed. Silent and calm. Coming from around the corner into the hallway is Trevor moved through the hall with pace. He reaches the elevator and enters. Going up toward the eighth floor. The agent waited as the elevator made its move. The steady stop and as the doors slid open, the Agent saw two well-dressed men standing in the hall, guarding a room. The Agent has found what he's searching for. He backed up to avoid being spotted. He reached down toward his side, revealing his *Ruger LCP.* Raising it slowly, prepared to fire. Before he continued his act, he glanced over to the wall in front of him, seeing a fire alarm. He paused. Thinking. He moved swiftly, pulling down the alarm and setting it off through the hall.

"The hell?" One of the men said.

"What do we do now?" The second man questioned.

"We keep this door secured. Nothing else matters right now."

"You're sure the alarm won't trigger anyone to come up this floor?"

"For what reason would anyone come up here uninvited? They want to die early?"

From the other rooms on the floor bolted out hotel guests.

Many of them. They make their way toward the stairs and the hallway is crowded. The Agent took a look, catching the hallway filled and the two men were still guarding the door. The guards themselves have their hand on their firearms for precaution. The Agent moved through the crowd without a misstep, placing a silencer over the muzzle to his Ruger. The Agent took the first shot before ducking down in midst of the crowd, The shot had killed one of the men as his body fell to the ground in the middle of the moving crowd. His partner turned over to look and noticed he wasn't standing on the other side.

"Where'd you go? We're on duty."

The Agent moved in closer as the hallway showed itself becoming empty. The Agent took the second shot, killing the second guard without fail. The Agent paused. He scouted the hallway, finding no one in sight besides the two dead guards. He nodded and opened the door. He walked into the room with his firearm in hand. Seeing it decorated with shelves of books, candles, and fancy décor. The Agent knew whoever had a room like this had the resources to acquire it. Discovering himself facing who's he come for. The target had been found. There was a man sitting at a desk, drinking a glass of scotch.

"Patrice O'Haire." The Agent said.

Patrice gestured his finger and from both side of the room emerged three more guards. Each with their firearms aimed at the Agent. The Agent glared toward each one of them, showing only an expression of a grin.

"If I only knew you were coming sooner I would've poured you a glass."

"Save yourself the favor. I'll drink after the mission is complete."

Patrice chuckled, laying back in the chair.

"You spies. You're all the same, you know. Always snooping around in others' business. A bit nosy don't you think. Strangely enough, you always wonder why no one wants to take a moment and leave you guys be."

"I'm not here to chat."

"I know. I know." Patrice smiled. "Tell me please, why have

you come to see me? What is it this time that has soured those on
the opposite sides of the work?"

"You know what you've done." The Agent answered. "No
need in repeating past words to rekindle your memory."

Patrice grunted.

"Again with this kind of talk. Do they teach you these words
in your training? My goodness! All business and no fun."

"You forget the work of a spy. The mission is always the fun
part."

"Sounds depressing." Patrice sighed. "Must be some kind of
life, huh?"

"It has its benefits."

"Indeed." Patrice nodded.

Patrice signaled his guards to prepare to fire. The Agent knew
the movements well, keeping his eyes locked on Patrice while
watching closely the motion of the guards. Six to one. The Agent
was confident in his abilities to succeed. Regardless of the
numbers.

"Any last words, Patrice?"

"Just a few." Patrice said, turning over to the guards. "Take
him."

The Agent gestured his eyes over to the opposite wall,
noticing a fire extinguisher. He shot the extinguisher, shrouding
the entire room in a fog. From there, he moved with silence
throughout the room. The guards scattered themselves searching
while Patrice remained at the desk, sitting down with concern.

"Shit!" Patrice yelled with a panic. "Find him! Kill him!"

The guards weren't able to see the Agent, yet he knew through
the fog where the guards were placed. The scenery reminded him
of target practice. From there, the Agent fired shots toward each
of them without a single stop in his step. Only the sounds of
thuds were heard through the white fog. Patrice couldn't see a
thing, waving his hand in the air. The fog had cleared, Patrice
found his desk surrounded by his guards, now dead on the floor,
bleeding into the carpet. The Agent however, was standing in
front of Patrice over the desk.

"I'm not going to repeat my last words."

Patrice jumped up from the chair, running out of the room toward the door to the hallway. The Agent followed him out. Patrice made a move to the elevator, even though the fire alarm was still buzzing. The Agent watched as Patrice panicked at the elevator with fear. Patrice stood by the elevator, vigorously pressing the button and yet, the elevator doors do not open. Patrice took another look behind, seeing the Agent walking toward him. Patrice fell on his knees, looking down in terror. The Agent removed the silencer

"This was the only way." The Agent said.

The Agent fired the shot, shooting Patrice in the head. Afterwards, the Agent placed his gun into its holster and reached for his phone. He dialed a number. Someone had answered on the other end.

"The mission is done. I'm on my way."

The Agent hung up, leaving the body of Patrice on the floor. The fire alarm had silenced just as the Agent pressed the elevator button and the doors opened. Going down to the first floor. The Agent made his way outside the hotel. He walked toward a silver sports car parked near the entrance. Taking out the keys from his jacket pocket, he entered the car. Driving from the hotel. The Agent drove through the streets, not far out from him was the city of Vancouver. The Agent took a turn, making his way toward the city's airport.

AGENT JOHN TREVOR WILL RETURN.

THE STORY OF ABELARD EKKEHARDT, ALLAN
DESPORTAN, LUCY SEWARD, ANNA IIARIO, BRANT WADE,
AND THE DARK ONE WILL CONTINUE IN:

THE
DREADED ONES

THE SECOND INSTALLMENT OF *THE HORDE* TRILOGY

ABOUT THE AUTHOR

Ty'Ron W. C. Robinson II is the author of several works of fiction. Including the *Dark Titan Universe Saga*, *The Haunted City Saga*, EverWar Universe, Symbolum Venatores, Frightened!, Instincts, and others. More information pertaining to the author and stories can be found at darktitanentertainment.com.

Twitter: @TyronRobinsonII

Twitter: @DarkTitan_
Instagram: @darktitanentertainment
Facebook: @DarkTitanEnt
Pinterest: @darktitanentertainment
YouTube: Dark Titan Entertainment